Jeremy
the Jet Plane

Based on *The Railway Series* **by the Rev. W. Awdry**

Illustrations by *Robin Davies and Jerry Smith*

EGMONT

EGMONT

We bring stories to life

First published in Great Britain 2008
This edition published in Great Britain 2013
by Egmont UK Limited
The Yellow Building, 1 Nicholas Road, London W11 4AN

Thomas the Tank Engine & Friends™

CREATED BY BRITT ALLCROFT
Based on the Railway Series by the Reverend W Awdry
© 2013 Gullane (Thomas) LLC. A HIT Entertainment company.
Thomas the Tank Engine & Friends and Thomas & Friends are trademarks of Gullane (Thomas) Limited.
Thomas the Tank Engine & Friends and Design is Reg. U.S. Pat. & Tm. Off.

HiT entertainment

ISBN 978 1 4052 6972 8
45461/13
Printed in Italy

Stay safe online. Egmont is not responsible for content hosted by third parties.

FSC
MIX
Paper
FSC® C018306

Egmont is passionate about helping to preserve the world's remaining ancient forests.
We only use paper from legal and sustainable forest sources.

This book is made from paper certified by the Forest Stewardship Council® (FSC®),
an organisation dedicated to promoting responsible management of forest resources.
For more information on the FSC, please visit www.fsc.org. To learn more about
Egmont's sustainable paper policy, please visit www.egmont.co.uk/ethical

This is a story about Jeremy, a splendid jet plane, who landed at Sodor Airport on the day of the summer picnic. Thomas was jealous of Jeremy until a rain storm broke out on the Island . . .

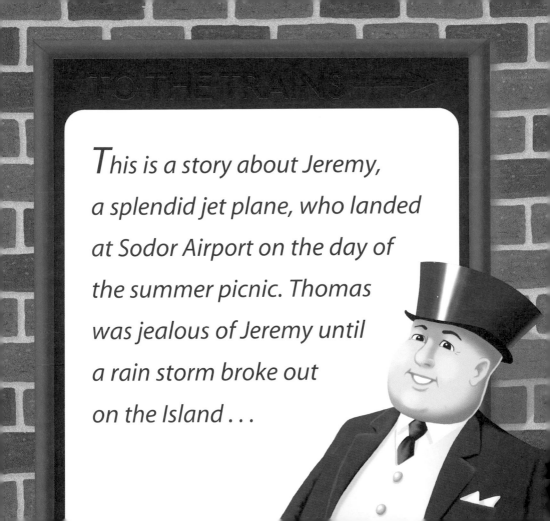

Thomas the Tank Engine loves having buffers that biff and a boiler that bubbles.

He loves having wheels that whizz round and round and a whistle that he can peep . . .

But most of all Thomas loves working on The Fat Controller's Railway.

It was the day of the Sodor Summer Picnic.

The Fat Controller came with news of a special job for Thomas. "You are to collect the children from the Airport, and take them to the picnic," he boomed, cheerfully.

Thomas was excited! "Yes, Sir," he whistled, and set off straight away.

The Airport was new and all the engines wanted to go there.

Thomas had just arrived, when he heard a loud noise in the sky. "Whoosh!"

A jet plane was coming in to land!

Thomas chuffed over to the big hangar. "Hello," he peeped. "I'm Thomas, and I'm a tank engine."

"Hello," said the plane. "I'm Jeremy and I'm a jet plane. Flying is the most fun in the world – I can see the whole Island at once," he said.

Thomas thought Jeremy was being boastful. "Well, I like travelling on tracks," he huffed.

Thomas puffed sadly away. "I never want to talk to a jet plane again!" he moaned.

He cheered up, though, when he saw the children waiting on the platform.

The Fat Controller and Lady Hatt were there, too, with a large hamper, full of delicious things to eat.

The Guard loaded the hamper into Clarabel.

Thomas set off for the picnic, but soon had to stop at a signal.

He heard Jeremy taking off. "Whoosh!"

Then Jeremy flew right over his funnel!

"It's not fair!" puffed Thomas. "Jet planes don't have to stop at signals."

At the picnic, everyone was soon having a jolly time. Everyone except Thomas.

Percy saw that he looked sad. "What's wrong, Thomas?" he asked.

"Jet planes can go wherever they like. I wish I were a jet plane," chuffed Thomas.

"But engines can pull carriages, and take children to picnics," peeped Percy. "Engines are Really Useful!"

Thomas wasn't so sure.

Jeremy was jetting to the Mainland, but dark rain clouds were gathering. Jeremy had to return to the Airport.

Thomas was passing, as Jeremy came in to land. Thomas didn't want to talk to him.

"Thomas!" Jeremy called out. "A summer storm is on its way, the picnic will be ruined!"

"Cinders and ashes!" gasped Thomas. "I must tell The Fat Controller."

Thomas steamed through tunnels and whizzed round bends. He reached the picnic just as the first drops of rain began to fall.

"Quickly!" he whooshed. "A big storm is coming. The picnic will be washed away!"

Everyone helped pack up the picnic and boarded Annie and Clarabel.

The children were sad that the picnic was over. Then Thomas had an idea. He steamed to the Airport, as fast as his wheels would carry him.

Jeremy was inside keeping nice and dry in his big hangar.

"Please can the children have their picnic here in your hangar?" asked Thomas.

"Of course," said Jeremy. "What a splendid idea!"

Thomas was very happy.

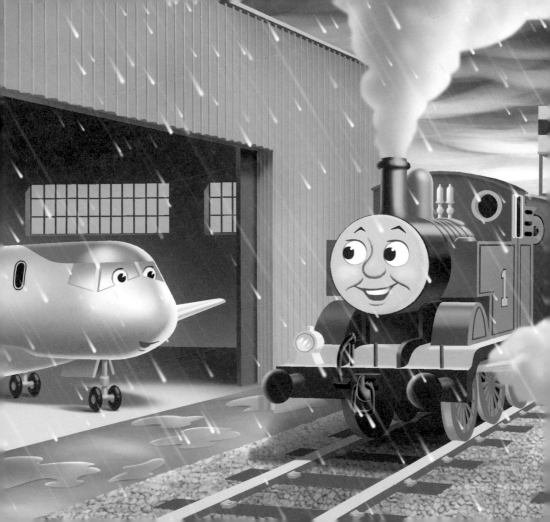

Soon, all the children were feeling jolly again. And so was The Fat Controller.

"Well done, Thomas and Jeremy!" he boomed. "Together you have saved the picnic. You are both Really Useful!"

Jeremy was happy to have helped.

And Thomas had never felt prouder to be a tank engine.

Now, whenever Thomas sees Jeremy flying high above him in the sky, he always whistles, "peep, peep!".

And Jeremy likes nothing better than looking out for Thomas, steaming along his branch line on the Island of Sodor.